SMALL BEAUTIES

The Journey of Darcy Heart O'Hara

BY

Elvira Woodruff

PICTURES BY

Adam Rex

Alfred A. Knopf
NEW YORK

FOR MY MOTHER, FRANNY PIROZZI, WHO ALWAYS NOTICED
THE WILDFLOWERS GROWING ALONG THE ROAD.

AND FOR THREE IRISH BEAUTIES I KNOW:
PAT M. BRISSON, WHO WAS BORN WITH POETRY IN HER SOUL,
CAROLINE RYON, WHO SHOWS HER HEART UPON HER PAGE,
& HER GRANDMOTHER, JOAN DONEGAN, WHOSE POETRY IS IN HER SMILE.
—E.W.

FOR EMMA LEEVER AND HER FAMILY—THANKS.
—A.R.

THIS IS A BORZOI BOOK PUBLISHED BY ALFRED A. KNOPF

Text copyright © 2006 by Elvira Woodruff
Illustrations copyright © 2006 by Adam Rex

Published in the United States by Alfred A. Knopf, an imprint of Random House Children's Books, a division of Random House, Inc., New York.

KNOPF, BORZOI BOOKS, and the colophon are registered trademarks of Random House, Inc.

www.randomhouse.com/kids

Educators and librarians, for a variety of teaching tools, visit us at
www.randomhouse.com/teachers

Library of Congress Cataloging-in-Publication Data
Woodruff, Elvira.
Small beauties : the journey of Darcy Heart O'Hara / by Elvira Woodruff ; pictures by Adam Rex. — 1st ed.
p.   cm.
SUMMARY: Darcy Heart O'Hara, a young Irish girl who neglects her chores to observe the beauties of nature and everyday life, shares
"family memories" with her homesick parents and siblings after the O'Haras are forced to immigrate to America in the 1840s.
ISBN: 0-375-82686-6 (trade) — ISBN: 0-375-92686-0 (lib. bdg.)
ISBN-13: 978-0-375-82686-3 (trade) — ISBN-13: 978-0-375-92686-0 (lib. bdg.)
1. Ireland—History—Famine, 1845–1852—Juvenile fiction. [1. Ireland—History—Famine, 1845–1852—Fiction.
2. Emigration and immigration—Fiction. 3. Family life—Ireland—Fiction.] I. Rex, Adam, ill. II. Title.
PZ7.W8606Sm 2006
[E]—dc22
2005016038

The illustrations in this book were created using charcoal and graphite pencils and oils on paper.

MANUFACTURED IN CHINA
10 9 8 7 6 5 4 3 2 1
First Edition

On the night Darcy O'Hara was born, her father danced a jig in the firelight of their small cottage. It was what fathers did long ago, in Ireland, in the cottages of Derry Lane, in the townland of Pobble O'Keefe.

"The babe has a gift, 'tis plain to see," Granny O'Hara whispered, her blue eyes twinkling. Granny herself had "second sight," which let her peek into the future.

The six O'Hara boys gathered round their new sister.

"One day this child shall hold the very heart of our family in the palm of her hand," Granny predicted.

So they named the infant Darcy Heart O'Hara.

Now children were as plentiful in Pobble O'Keefe as the chickens that roosted in the thatched roofs up and down Derry Lane. But Darcy was different. She was a noticer. She stopped to notice small beauties wherever she went.

"Darcy Heart O'Hara, how many times must you be told to milk the cow?" Granny would call from the half door. "Whatever are you doing while our Kathleen is waitin' so patient?"

"'Tis a grand sight I see, Granny," Darcy would answer, pointing to a dew-covered spiderweb across her bucket's rim.

"It won't be a grand sight you'll be seeing if your father hasn't milk for his tea," Granny snapped.

"Darcy Heart
O'Hara!" her mother
would call up to the roof.
"I sent you up to gather
eggs ages ago. What
keeps you, girl?"

"I'm on my way,
Mam," Darcy was
quick to call down.
"I just stopped to watch
the cloud castles," she
said, pointing to the sky.

"Clouds, is it?" her
mother would fume.
"I can't be using clouds
to barter with in the
market. Gather up those
eggs and hurry down!"

Now the O'Haras, like many of their neighbors, knew more about courage than coin. For in Pobble O'Keefe, in the year 1845, money was as rare as a whortleberry in December.

Darcy's dress had neither collar nor pocket. But as poor as she was, Darcy often felt rich with the many beauties she noticed. And when she could, she liked to carry the smallest ones home in the hem of her skirt. She'd carefully pull a few stitches loose and tuck in a flower,

a pebble,

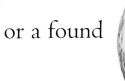
or a found   butterfly's wing.

*I*n the evenings, with kittens curled in laps, dogs flopped over feet, and piglets poking about, the O'Haras would gather at the hearth.

There they listened to stories, the kind only Granddad could spin. With a low, hushy whisper, he'd begin,

"Long ago, on our fair Isle of Erin . . ." In the glow of the peat fire, Darcy noticed how Granddad's voice would rise and fall as he told of brave heroes on white steeds and moonlit glens

filled with little folk and fairy queens.

The children would gasp and gape and the piglets would grunt in all the right places. All together, at the hearth, they were happy, and Darcy noticed.

But such happiness was not to last. For the summer brought nothing but "soft weather," as Granny called the rain. And when the sun finally did come out, Darcy walked with her father over the soggy fields to inspect their crop of potatoes. The lush green leaves had curled and turned black. The potatoes had all gone rotten! It was the same in every field, in every county, all over Ireland.

"How shall we pay the rent?" Darcy's mother cried. "And what shall we feed the children?"

"We'll do the only thing we can," Darcy's father answered. "We'll plant more potatoes and pray our luck changes. Everyone shall help with the planting."

"Darcy Heart O'Hara, what in heaven's name are you doing dawdling in that empty row?" her brother Sean scolded.

"I was just noticing a magpie flying low over the buttercups," Darcy told him as she pointed to the edge of the field. "See how his black feathers shine next to their shimmering gold."

"Gold, is it?" her brother cried. "Why can't you ever see what the rest of us see? If you did, you'd notice that there's no gold here, just a bunch of useless blossoms. Stop gaping over buttercups now and get back to your planting."

But the next crop of potatoes turned as rotten as the first, for a blight had taken hold of the land. Now the hard times were certainly upon them. Each day Darcy joined the other children of Pobble O'Keefe, who were sent out looking for food. They combed the fields for berries and nettles, and whatever else they could find.

Darcy tried hard to take her brother's advice, to see what the others saw. She saw the worried look on her mother's face, and she noticed the hungry tug in the pit of her own stomach each day. She saw the rubble where the Murphys' cottage had once stood. She noticed the smell of rotten potatoes in the air. And she heard the quiet all up and down Derry Lane, as fiddles lay forgotten and stories were left untold.

ut even with all this, Darcy continued to notice
small beauties wherever she went.

When the Crown's agent came demanding the rent, Mr. O'Hara explained they couldn't pay it. The agent grabbed hold of their cow, Kathleen, and all of their pigs as well!

Darcy felt a lump in her throat to hear her father plead, "If you take our animals, my children will starve."

"What's owed is owed," the agent said gruffly. "The Crown's decided to clear the land. If you can't pay your rent, you're to be evicted. There's been a decree that all tenants of Pobble O'Keefe shall receive free passage to America if they leave within the month. If you haven't left by then, we'll come tear your house down."

"America!" Mrs. O'Hara cried.

"Cross the ocean?" Granny gasped.

"Leave Ireland?" Darcy whispered.

"Never!" declared Granddad. "We'll not leave the land our people are buried in. You'll not be rid of us so easy."

"There's hope from the ocean, but none from the grave," the agent said darkly.

*I*n the afternoons, Darcy and Granny took to saying their prayers together under the shade of the mulberry tree. While Granny fingered her worn wooden rosary beads, Darcy would finger the bumps along her hem. They prayed for food and for courage. And they prayed that the agent would not return.

*B*ut this last prayer went unanswered, for at the end of the month the Crown's agent was again at their door. And this time he was not alone. With him were men with hooks, hammers, and a torch!

Darcy trembled to hear the agent's angry voice shouting through the half door.

"Patrick O'Hara, I'm here to serve you notice. You and yours are evicted from this place, from this day forward. Take what you will from your house now, for it's coming down."

With her own heart breaking, Darcy watched helplessly as Granny's rosary beads fell from the mantel and broke on the floor!

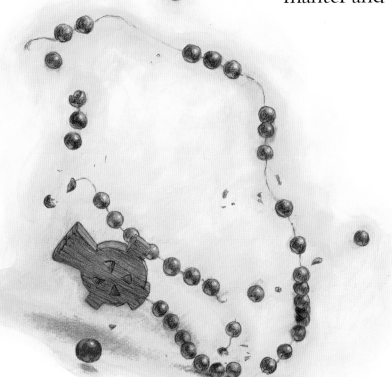

"Heaven protect us! They've set the roof afire!" Granddad cried as the sound of burning thatch crackled in their ears overhead. In a panic, everyone rushed for the only door. Amid the smoke and screams, Darcy reached down and scooped up one small bead from the floor.

Outside she placed it into Granny's trembling hand.

That night, as the stars twinkled over the moss-covered stones along Derry Lane, the O'Haras huddled in a ditch beside the rubble that was once their home.

"There's nothing left for us here." Mrs. O'Hara's voice was a weary whisper in the wind.

"We must take the Crown's tickets and cross the ocean," Mr. O'Hara said sadly. "There's a group leaving tomorrow. In America, there is food and there is the chance to own land. We'll leave at first light."

But Granddad shook his head. "Your Granny and I are too old to make such a journey. We'll stay here in Ireland if my sister Mag will take us in."

They spoke no more, for the sadness in their hearts was now too heavy for words.

Early the next morning, Darcy awoke before the others.
Silently she stepped around the ruins of what had once
been their home. She peeked into
the rubble and searched through
the stones, until she noticed
something special. She
quietly opened her hem
and slipped the small
beauty in.

ater that day, Darcy took one last walk with Granny down Derry Lane. "'Tis a big ocean that will soon be between us," Granny whispered, a tear rolling down her wrinkled cheek. "And the years will come and go like so many waves upon the shore. I'm countin' on you, my girl, you who notice so much. With all those small beauties you keep, here is one more." She pressed the worn bead back into Darcy's hand. "Help the others to remember, and not just the sadness, the hurt, and the hunger. Help them to remember all the beauty they left behind."

"But I don't want to go, Gran!" Darcy sobbed. "I want to stay here with you."
"Oh, my little one," Granny sighed. "I know, I know."

Now there is no farewell sadder than the farewell of forever, and so it was with many tears that the O'Haras bid their beloved Ireland good-bye. They traveled by foot and by cart, by ferry and by boat. The seas were rough and people were crowded close belowdecks. Darcy covered her face with her scarf to keep the stink from her nose as the ship pitched to and fro on the choppy sea.

After many long weeks of travel, the family finally crossed the wide ocean to America. Darcy found the island of Manhattan very different from the island she had known.

Where's the heather? she wondered. *Where's the bog?*

Instead of tiny cottages, Darcy saw tall buildings stretched to the sky. Instead of fields of rotting potatoes, she noticed shops and carts overflowing with fresh fruits and vegetables. Instead of barefoot children dressed in rags, she saw girls and boys wearing hats, coats, and shoes! Everything was different. Everything was new. And best of all was the hope that the family could one day buy land of their own.

But for all the newness, Darcy remembered the old. The first week in their new country found the O'Haras gathered together around a smoky little stove in a cramped city cellar. They were worn and weary, tired to the bone. And as they talked of their day and the days to come, Darcy silently began to loosen the stitches of her hem.

"What have we here?" her father asked, looking up from his pipe.

Darcy smiled as she pulled out her small beauties from home. First came a little round pebble covered in moss.

Next came a magpie's feather, black as night.

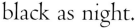

There were dried blossoms of buttercups,

dog violets,

and heather too.

"*Ach mucha.* Dear me." Mother gasped at the sight of the old wooden bead from Granny's rosary.

A hush fell over the family then as they watched Darcy next pull a little chip of slate from her hem.

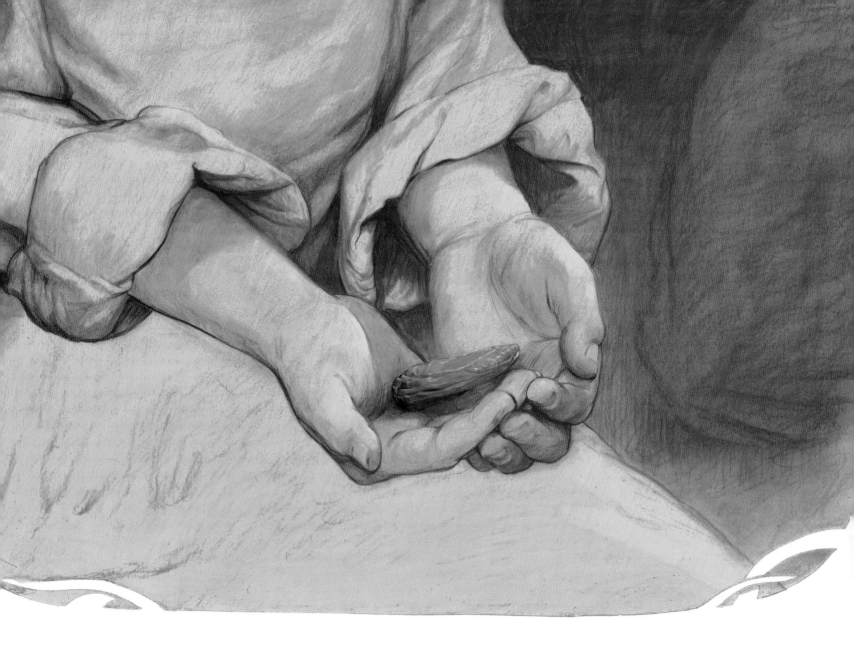

"And what is that one there?" her brothers whispered, leaning in close.
"'Tis a bit of our hearthstone," she told them, holding the chip in her palm.
And suddenly the old familiar smell of a peat fire was in the air. They could hear Granny humming to the baby and the creak of her chair. They heard their own laughter as the piglets squealed. And soon the hushy whisper of Granddad's voice filled their ears. "Long ago, on our fair Isle of Erin . . ."

And so it was that Granny O'Hara's prediction came to be true, for those small beauties that Darcy held in her hand called up the very memories her family held most dear. And Darcy Heart O'Hara went right on noticing.

Author's Note:

While Darcy and her family sprung from my imagination, the spark for their story came from my reading about a very real family who was forced to leave Ireland during the famine.

They left County Cork in 1847, sailing first to Canada and then on to America. Sadly, the mother of this family died aboard ship, but her children survived and settled with their father in Michigan. One son, William, went on to marry and have a son of his own called Henry.

This boy loved to tinker with the machines on the farm, and he grew up to become one of the forefathers of American industry. But his family's memories of fleeing the famine were very much a part of who Henry was, despite his success and fame.

Years later, he traveled to Ireland. A millionaire many times over, he could have afforded the most precious of gems—diamonds, rubies, and more. And yet what stone did he choose to ship back to America? A worthless old hearthstone removed from a humble cottage—worthless to some, but priceless to Henry Ford, for it was the very hearthstone that his father's family had gathered around the night before they were to leave Ireland forever.

Henry Ford, whose "horseless carriage," the automobile, changed the landscape of America, understood the importance of family memory. I hope you will too. And just as Darcy did, take the time to notice the small beauties you have all around you. For one day you may find that they are the very memories you treasure most.